Disney
Baby Bluebird

Written by
Guy Davis

Illustrated by
Art Mawhinney

Published by
Louis Weber, C.E.O., Publications International, Ltd.
7373 North Cicero Avenue, Lincolnwood, Illinois 60712

Ground Floor, 59 Gloucester Place, London W1U 8JJ

Customer Service: 1-800-595-8484 or customer_service@pilbooks.com

www.pilbooks.com

p i kids is a registered trademark of Publications International, Ltd.

Manufactured in China.
ISBN-13: 978-1-4127-3020-4
ISBN-10: 1-4127-3020-1

"Hmmm, now what could this be?" wondered Winnie the Pooh. He had been enjoying a splendid walk through the Hundred-Acre Wood when he discovered something he hadn't seen before.

Pooh had found a nest on the ground with a round, smooth *something* sitting inside.

Pooh needed someone wise to help him solve this mystery.

So it was very lucky that Owl, who was very wise indeed, just happened to be walking by. Owl stopped to say hello.

Owl was only too happy to help. He loved solving a good mystery!

"I say, my dear boy, what you have here is a very rare whozit!" declared Owl, studying the egg intently. "But you must be very careful with a whozit because...."

Before Owl could finish, there was a loud *c-c-c-r-r-rack* from the egg.

The egg hatched, and out popped a tiny creature! Before Owl could say anything, the little whozit let out a great, big *peep!* In fact, the whozit made so much noise that soon Rabbit joined them to find out what was going on.

"The whozit is trying to tell us something," said Owl. "I may be a bear of very little brain," said Pooh, "but I think this little whozit is telling us he's a little hungry."

"What does a whozit like to eat?" wondered Rabbit.

"Why, honey, of course," Pooh answered. "What else?"

Oddly, the whozit didn't want the honey. Instead, he peeped louder!

"No, no, no," said Rabbit. "Honey is much too sweet for a little baby whozit. Everyone knows that whozits like vegetables."

Rabbit dashed back to his garden and returned with a basket full of carrots. "Here you go, little whozit," said Rabbit. "Here's a nice, delicious carrot!"

The baby whozit turned his head away and peeped even louder.

"My dear fellows, you are both wrong," said Owl. "This is a *baby* whozit. Everyone knows that babies like milk." Owl raced off and came back with a nice tall glass of milk.

The baby whozit turned his head
away, flapped his wings, and let out
an even louder *peep!*

Pooh, Owl, and Rabbit had run
out of ideas. They were stumped.
    Suddenly, they heard a sweet little
peep-peep-peep from up above. It
was the baby whozit's mother sitting
on a tree branch!
    "It looks like the baby's mother has
something in her beak," said Rabbit.

The baby's mother flew down and landed softly beside her son. He was very excited to see her, especially when she fed him the worm she held in her beak.

The friends all cheered as the whozit stopped peeping and snuggled up next to his mother.

"I say, it appears that their nest fell out of the tree!" said Owl. "We must help put it back." And that's just what they did.

"It's amazing," said Pooh. "These whozits sure look like bluebirds."